OGRES
Don't
DANCE

KIRSTY MCKAY

Andersen Press

First published in 2014 by
Andersen Press Limited
20 Vauxhall Bridge Road
London SW1V 2SA
www.andersenpress.co.uk

2 4 6 8 10 9 7 5 3 1

British Library Cataloguing in Publication Data available.

ISBN 978 1 84939 715 5

Printed and bound in Great Britain
by CPI Group UK (Ltd), Croydon CR0 4YY

OGRES Don't DANCE

For Xanthe,
Who loves to dance

Ogden the Ogre was trundling back home after a particularly successful supper. He had eaten two fat schoolteachers, a juicy greengrocer and a delightfully crunchy nun.

As the sun set behind the snow-capped mountains, the big, green ogre left the lonely village far behind, heading for home and sleepy wink-winks. He loved his new, cosy cave in the woods. This was just as well, because he had been chased out of his last home by a horde of stick-flinging humans. Stick-flinging humans can be

1

very tricky, so Ogden had chosen a cave deep in the forest, hidden away.

Very well hidden . . . Ogden crinkled his green brow, and sniffed the air. Something was wrong. Very wrong.

Ogden the Ogre was lost.

He peered through the dark trees. Wherever had his cave gone?

'Uh-oh!' he sighed. 'Ogden so full and sleepy!'

There was nothing else for it. He rubbed his hairy belly and lay down on a bracken patch to snooze. All was quiet; the birds snuggled into their nests and the moles snored deep in their holes.

But not for long.

'Cha-cha-cha! Cha-cha-cha!'

Ogden sat up with a jolt. What was that?

'Rumpty, pumpty, bump-bump-bump!'

Ogden got up and squinted into the distance.

'Trumpa-pumpa, la, la, la!'

'Happy sounds!' Ogden smiled a crinkly smile and clapped his huge green hands. He forgot how tired he was. The funny noises made him want to jiggle and wiggle

3

and shake his big behind.

He spotted a brightly lit building nestled amongst the knobbly oak trees, and slowly tippy-tiptoed up to a window. There, inside a large room, were lots and lots of . . . humans.

Some of the humans were strumming strings and blowing things.

'Make happy sounds!' Ogden gasped, pointing.

And dozens of humans were whirling across the floor in time to the happy sounds, wearing dazzling clothes of every colour.

'Ooh, sparkles!' Ogden cooed.

There were humans jumping up and down. There were humans holding one another while they pranced around the room. There were humans tap-tapping their feet. Ogden had never seen humans do these kinds of things before. What was going on?

Ogden tickled his bald head, and thought some thoughts.

The humans smelled extremely tasty to Ogden, but he was already so very full. And if he ate these humans, there would be no more happy sounds and sparkles.

Ogden felt confused.

Just as the happy sounds finished, he let out a loud **burp**. All the humans looked at the window, and Ogden quickly ducked out of sight.

'Uh-oh!' he said. 'Ogden run away quickly-quick!' He scarpered into the forest. After many twists and turns, he finally found his cave. He went to sleep and dreamed smiley dreams about the happy sounds, the sparkles and the jumping up and down.

★

The next evening, Ogden hummed as he strolled back to his cave from the village. His tum was extremely full. He'd nibbled a niggly nanny and gobbled a grumpy grandpa. Now it was time for sleeps and dreams. But as he passed the bracken patch, he heard a noise floating through the forest. It was a noise he recognised:

'Rumpa-thumpa, oom-pah-pah!'

Ogden smiled a crinkly smile.

'Happy sounds!'

He followed the noise, and found himself back at the brightly lit building, where he peeped through the window, quietly. There were the humans again! Jumping up and down! Chasing each other around the room, in sparkly clothes!

Ogden spied a little man standing on a stage at one end of the room. As the happy sounds came to an end, the man shouted at the other humans.

'Take your partners for the final dance!'

'Dance,' Ogden whispered. He frowned as he thought some thoughts.

'Ogden want to dance.'

The happy sounds started again. As Ogden looked through the window, he began to tap his feet, his long toenails click-clicking on the path. He wanted to go in there – not to eat the humans, but to dance with them. Could he dance too?

Ogden thought some more thoughts.

'Ogres don't dance.' Ogden sighed, and shuffled back to his cave, scuffing his big, gnarly feet on the ground.

The next night, Ogden's tum was gurgly. He'd munched a mouldy farmer with a prickly-tickly beard. Ogden burped, loudly. No more supper for him today.

On his way home, he began to think a thought. And the thought wouldn't go away. He wandered through the forest until he reached the brightly lit building where the happy sounds had been coming from the evening before. 'Dance!' He wrinkled his big chops into a grin.

The sounds became louder and louder as he got closer. Almost as if a spell had been cast on him, his huge feet began to tap, his hairy shoulders began to shake, and his big behind jiggled in time to the music. Ogden knew what he had to do. This time, there was no going back.

He spied a door, crept up to it and flung it open. 'Who will dance with Ogden?' he bellowed.

All the humans stopped dancing and the happy sounds stopped too. Ogden turned to a lady with a peacock feather in her hair. He grinned an ogre grin, baring his huge teeth. And asked in his politest voice: 'Will you dance with me?'

'**Aaaargh!**' screamed the lady and fell over in a dizzy swoon.

Everyone shouted, 'Run for your lives!' and scurried around in circles, their arms in the air.

'Is this another dance?' said Ogden, waving his arms too.

The humans squealed like piglets, skibbling through the door and jumping out of the windows.

'Don't go!' Ogden shouted after them.

But they did.

Ogden hung his head and sighed. 'Only want to dance,' he mumbled, picking a pink feather boa off the floor and hanging it round his neck. He left the dance hall and started to walk home to his cave, the feather boa tickling him under the nose.

'Nobody want to dance with Ogden,' he said sadly. 'Lonely old lump I am.' With this, he let out a howl, sank to his knees underneath a knobbly oak tree and began to cry hot tears.

A voice came from above him. 'What's all the racket?'

In the dusky light, Ogden looked up.

Nestling in the branches of the knobbly oak was a tree house. Through the branches Ogden could see a girl in the tree house, a girl with yellow hair and wearing striped pyjamas. She was holding a lantern up to her face and looking out into the night air.

'You down there, keep quiet!' The girl rubbed her eyes. 'Can't you let a person sleep?'

But Ogden was too upset to care, and boo-ed and hoo-ed all the more loudly.

'Right, that's it!' said the girl. 'I'm coming to shut you up!' She appeared at the top of a ladder, the lantern clanking on the rungs as she climbed down. 'No consideration for others, it's so rude!' She stopped at the bottom of the tree, held her lantern high, and peered at Ogden through the gloomy night air.

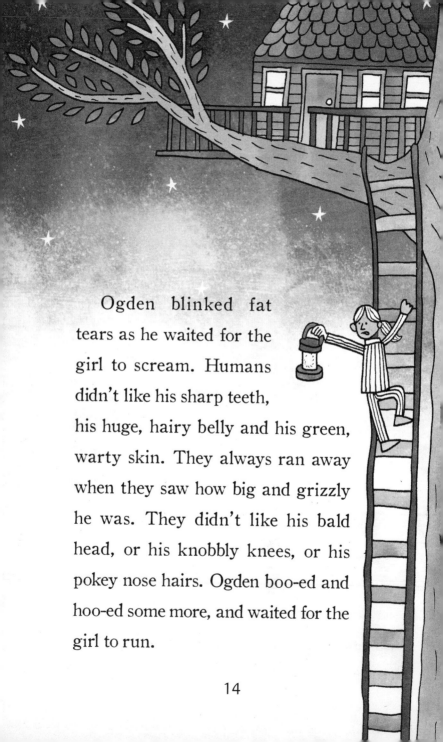

Ogden blinked fat tears as he waited for the girl to scream. Humans didn't like his sharp teeth, his huge, hairy belly and his green, warty skin. They always ran away when they saw how big and grizzly he was. They didn't like his bald head, or his knobbly knees, or his pokey nose hairs. Ogden boo-ed and hoo-ed some more, and waited for the girl to run.

But she didn't. She blinked back at him, and rubbed her eyes, as if she was dreaming.

'You . . . you're an ogre!' she gasped.

Ogden nodded. 'Sad, sad ogre.'

The girl quickly grabbed the bottom of the ladder. 'Are you going to eat me?'

Ogden shook his head. 'Don't eat child-humans. Them too-too skinny and wiggly.'

'Are you sure about that?' The girl narrowed her eyes.

Ogden nodded. 'You weeny-tiny.'

'I'm not weeny-tiny, I'm nine years old!' She frowned at him. 'But I'm glad you don't want to eat me, or I would have to clonk you with this lantern.' She let go of the ladder and took a small step towards him. 'Why are you crying?'

Ogden sobbed and blubbed. 'Only

wanted to dance. Everyone ran away. No more happy sounds and sparkles!'

The girl stared at him and burst out laughing. She hugged her ribs and roared so hard that Ogden thought she might split in two. He scratched his head. No human had ever laughed at him before. This was a very strange girl.

She finally stopped laughing. 'You're a *dancing* ogre?' she said.

'Name is Ogden,' said Ogden, holding out his gnarly hand.

'Pleased to meet you, Ogden,' said the girl, shaking his hand. 'My name is Willow. I like your pink feather boa. It really suits you.'

'Thank you, Willow.'

'So nobody would dance with you?' she asked.

Ogden shook his head sadly. 'Everyone afraid I eat them.'

'Well, yes, that would explain it,' said Willow. 'If you really want someone to dance with, the very first thing you should do is to stop eating people.'

'*Really* want to dance,' said Ogden shyly.

Willow folded her arms. 'Faithfully promise never to eat another human being . . . and I will dance with you.'

The ogre stared back at her.

'Willow dance with Ogden?'

Willow nodded. 'Luckily for you, I'm on my summer holidays. No one comes to my tree house, so we'll have all the time we need. I'll teach you to dance if you swear never to munch another person again. Do we have a deal?'

Ogden thought some thoughts.

'We have a deal,' he said. 'But what about Ogden's hungry tum?'

'I've got just the thing,' Willow said, climbing the ladder to her tree house.

A moment later, three hard round things landed **Plop! Plop! Plop!** beside Ogden in the soft grass. He picked one up and sniffed it suspiciously. It was a tin of cat food! Was this Willow's idea of a meal?

'Meet me here tomorrow after breakfast and we'll have our first lesson,' shouted Willow from the treetop.

Ogden gathered up his feather boa and cat food. Would Willow be true to her promise and teach him to dance, or was it some kind of trick? Humans could be so very tricksy. He looked up and saw Willow's face poke through the branches.

'And don't be late!'

Ogden barely slept a wink that night.

He was so excited about his dance lesson with Willow it made his tum feel giggly. When the sun came up, he stared at the three tins Willow had given him for his breakfast. *Chomp-a-Lot Cat Food for Fabulous Felines!* it said on the label. Ogden tossed the cat food into his mouth, cans and all.

'Not bad,' he burped.

He wrapped the pink feather boa around his neck and set off through the forest. As he went on his way he saw a group of woodcutters sitting on a fallen tree, eating their breakfast. How good they smelled! He would have given anything to eat a couple of them. He began to creep towards them . . . but then he thought about his deal with Willow.

'No more humans, just Chomp-a-Lot!' he said to himself. He turned to go, but it was too late, the woodcutters had seen him . . .

'Run for your lives! An ogre!' They threw huge sticks at Ogden and scattered in all directions.

'Ogden won't eat you!' shouted Ogden. But the men had gone. Ogden sniffed the air. The men had left something behind: a pork pie, a scrumptious crumpet and a pickled egg.

'More breakfast!' said Ogden, scoffing

the lot. Human food didn't taste too bad after all.

When he reached the clearing, there was music coming out of Willow's tree house. 'Happy sounds!' he cried, and clapped his gnarly hands.

Willow leaned over the edge of the tree house deck. She was wearing blue dungarees with patches on the knees, and her blonde hair was tied back in a knot on her head. In her hands was a black box. Ogden squinted at it. The happy sounds were coming from the box!

The girl looked down at him.

'So you turned up? Before I come down, I want to know if you have kept your part of the deal.'

'No humans!' said Ogden, proudly beating his chest, 'Only ate Chomp-a-Lot!'

'Well done!' beamed Willow.

'And my breakfast of woodcutters,' said Ogden, baring his enormous, sharp teeth.

Willow's face froze. 'You ate woodcutters?'

'No! I ate their breakfast!' said Ogden, winking at her.

'Cheeky ogre!' said Willow as she climbed down to him, the music box tucked under her arm.

'Pixies inside?' said Ogden, pointing to the box. 'The fairy folk play happy sounds for us?'

Willow chuckled. 'Ogden, it's a radio.' She placed the box on the soft, green grass. 'Well, with all that breakfast, you'll be bursting with energy. We'll begin with exercises.'

'Exercises?' said Ogden.

23

Willow looked at him sharply. 'If you're going to be a dancer, you'll have to know how to wake up your muscles before we start the lesson. What exercises do you know?'

Ogden thought some thoughts.

'Running,' he said at last.

'Running!' Willow clapped her hands. 'That's excellent!'

'Running after tasty humans for to catch 'em!' Ogden nodded, then his face fell as he remembered his promise.

Willow raised an eyebrow at him. 'From now on we'll just run on the spot. Like this.' She started to jog, her knees high in the air.

Ogden copied her. The earth trembled. Birds were shaken out of their nests, and moles were bounced out of their holes.

'Don't forget to point your toes, dancer!' shouted Willow.

Ogden tried to point his toes, but landed on the ground with a thump. Willow stared at him lying on the grass.

'What's wrong with your feet?' she said.

'Og got wrong feets?' asked Ogden, waggling them at her.

'You've got two *left* feet!' Willow exclaimed. 'How on earth are we going to teach you to dance with two left feet?' She put her head in her hands.

'Can't dance with wrong feets,' Ogden said, and a big tear rolled down his leathery cheek.

'A dancer never gives up!' said Willow. 'I've got an idea!' She clambered up the ladder to her tree house.

Ogden waited.

Plop! Plop! Something was falling from above!

There in the grass lay two tiny bottles, one gold and one silver. Ogden picked them up carefully and sniffed them. 'More cat food?' he murmured.

'Do you think of nothing but your stomach?' Willow asked, appearing at his side. 'Give me one of your feet.' Willow slowly unscrewed the top from the gold bottle. A small brush was attached to the lid and she dipped it into the bottle, up and down, until the brush was covered in glittery gold liquid.

'Sparkles!' cried Ogden, his face screwing up with pleasure.

'Toe sparkles,' said Willow, smiling as she painted Ogden's toenails with the varnish. 'Eww, Ogden! Your feet

smell of squeezy cheese! Do you ever clean your toenails?'

'Never,' said Ogden proudly, offering her his other foot. Willow unscrewed the silver bottle and painted the rest of the nails quickly.

'There! Gold for your left-left foot and silver for your right-left foot! Now you'll always know which is which.'

'Pretty!' said Ogden gleefully, lying on his back twiddling his glamorous toes in the warm breeze.

'No time for lying around, dancer!' barked Willow. 'We've got to start working.'

And work they did.

Willow showed Ogden the steps of a dance called the cha-cha.

'One-two-three, gold foot forward!

One-two-three, silver foot forward!'
Willow shouted, as they danced together.
'Stand up straight! Don't look down!'

'Wheeeeeeeee!' said Ogden.

In no time at all Ogden and Willow
were prancing around the clearing. They
were so excited that they didn't notice an
eerie quiet settle over the wood as all the
animals and birds hid away in their homes.
They didn't notice a chilly wind blowing
large, black clouds over the sun.

Something was coming.

'Time for lunch!' panted Willow.

She laid a red-and-white checked tablecloth on the grass and set out a fine feast of crusty bread, creamy cheese and juicy berries. 'Dig in!' she said to Ogden.

Ogden wrinkled his nose. 'These is your foods?'

'And yours too, Og,' said Willow. 'If you eat the right things, they'll make you twirl faster, jump higher, dance better.'

Ogden nodded, seriously. 'Want to dance better.' He delicately picked out a single berry and popped it in his mouth. The flavour exploded with a **POP!** on his tongue – it was so tasty. He tried a handful more. 'Willow,' he said thoughtfully, his mouth full. 'Yesterday, you gave me foods for cats. Where are these cats?'

'They've gone.' Willow shook her head, sadly. 'Their names were Spanky, Furtle and Nog. They were wild. One day they appeared at the bottom of the ladder, just like you did – in fact, they made almost as much noise as you, meowing for grub! They lived here with me for a few weeks, but then one day they disappeared.'

'Where dids they go?' Ogden asked.

Willow shrugged. 'I don't know. The tree house feels quite empty without them.'

Ogden patted Willow's shoulder. 'Don't be lonely, Little Will. Maybe Og will be your new friend?'

Willow smiled. 'I hope so.' She pulled a face at him. 'That's if he doesn't eat me first!'

'No!' Ogden was shocked. 'Ogden no eat humans ever-never again!'

'I trust you,' Willow said.

Ogden was happily tucking into his third helping of bread and cheese, when a weird whiff floated through the air. He leaped to his feet.

Willow jumped in shock. 'What's wrong?' Then she screwed up her face. 'Pooey! What is that smell?'

Ogden quickly grabbed her round the waist and bounded towards the tree house.

'What are you doing?' Willow cried.

'Shush!' said Ogden, carrying her up the creaking ladder. 'Danger-monsters!'

Willow's eyes widened. The tree house swayed under Ogden's weight. He carefully put Willow down and lay flat out on the deck. He pointed through the branches down to the clearing where a moment ago the two had been eating their lunch. As Willow watched, three large, orange, furry mounds crept from the trees and moved towards the tablecloth.

'Fleshfeasting Fluffy Grocklers!' whispered Ogden.

'Fleshfeasting what? Whatever they are, they don't half pong,' Willow whispered back, holding her nose. 'Wet dog and mouldy leaves!' She looked down at the clearing. 'I've never seen them before. Apart from a couple of pesky pixies and a wheezy old troll, we don't get many monsters this close to the village. Oh – and you.'

'Ssh!' Ogden held his finger up to his mouth. 'We must be quietly-quiet now.'

Below them, the Fluffy Grocklers snuffled at the food. They had thick orange fur with bald patches and googly eyes with fierce dark brows that met in the middle. Their noses were long and pointy and their mouths were dribbly. Quickly they moved around the clearing on huge, hairy feet, muttering to themselves and scratching at the ground like demented chickens.

'I don't think they want our lunch, do they?' whispered Willow.

'Them want flesh and blood and crunchy bones!' said Ogden, his eyes blazing.

'Yuck,' said Willow. 'Well, they're not having any of my crunchy bones.'

Suddenly, the Fluffy Grocklers stopped and sniffed the air. Slowly they moved towards the tree house, with their pointy wet noses held high.

Willow flattened herself against the deck of the tree house and shut her eyes. Ogden squeezed her hand gently as the Grocklers came closer.

A single pink feather from Ogden's feather boa drifted across the floor towards Willow and tickled her on the nose.

Willow sat up and sneezed.

'Aaa . . . aaa . . . tish-oo!'

The Grocklers looked into the trees.
Ogden and Willow held their breath. The
biggest Fluffy Grockler let out a high-
pitched scream and jumped up and down
on the spot. To the pair's horror, they saw
the three monsters were making their way
towards the tree house ladder.

'Ogden!' Willow pointed at the hatch in
the floor. 'They're going to find us!'

Ogden leaped to his feet and grabbed a box of the Chomp-a-Lot tins.

He opened the hatch and emptied them all on top of the monsters.

Bop! Bop! Bop!

The cat food landed on the Grocklers' heads and knocked them to the ground. Before they had time to think, Ogden bounded down from the tree house and stood before them on the grass.

'**Rooooaaaaaaaarrrrrhhh!**' he cried.

The biggest Fluffy Grockler slowly rose to its full height and pawed at the grass with its huge foot, like a bull about to charge. Ogden quickly took the pink feather boa from his neck and tied a can of cat food to one end. He swung it round his head and just as the monster rushed at him, he let go! The tin hit the monster square on its pointy wet nose and sent it crashing to the ground.

'Go, Ogden!' yelled Willow.

The second Grockler ran at Ogden, but the ogre quickly spun out of the way, sending the furry fiend into the tree trunk with a **Thwack!**

The third and littlest monster trembled in fright and backed onto the red and white tablecloth.

'Grrrrrrrrrrrr!'

Ogden growled menacingly at the littlest Grockler and whipped the cloth from underneath its feet, making it fall on its behind with a squeal.

Ogden beat his chest with his gnarly fists and roared, 'Away, you Fleshfeasting Fluffies! This my tree house! This my human! Away and don't come back!'

With that, the Fluffy Grocklers limped and lollopped away as fast as their huge orange feet would carry them.

Ogden waited a moment, sniffed the air and said to Willow, 'Safe now.'

Willow climbed down the ladder and looked around nervously. 'Are you sure they won't come back?' she asked. 'My aunty will never let me stay out here if she knows there are monsters around.'

'Won't come back now,' Ogden said. 'Them think Ogden live here. Scared of big ogre.' He sat down on a tree stump, exhausted.

'Clever Ogden!' cried Willow, flinging her arms around his neck and kissing him on the cheek. 'You saved my life, you brave, brave ogre! How can I ever thank you?'

Ogden blushed as red as the red and white tablecloth.

'More dancing lessons?' he said.

Each day Ogden visited Willow at the tree house. He kept his promise not to eat any more humans, although sometimes it was very hard indeed.

One afternoon, a hunter wandered near his cave. He smelled so good that Ogden dribbled down his chin! Another time, Ogden spotted a washerwoman by the stream who looked so fat and delicious that Ogden had to eat ten tins of cat food and hum happy sounds until he felt better.

And he did feel better. Every day he

loved his dancing more and more, and every day it got a little easier not to eat humans.

A couple of weeks later, to thank Willow for the dancing lessons, Ogden decided to invite her to his cave for a surprise dinner. He set a large slab of stone on the grass in front, and put a huge tablecloth over the plates of food he had prepared. It was a warm evening, and the light breeze carried the sweet scent of woodland flowers. Birds twittered in the trees overhead, and Ogden nibbled his fingernails nervously as he waited for Willow to appear.

Willow arrived on time, wearing her best pair of yellow dungarees. 'All that dancing has made me very hungry!' she said, sitting down on the soft grass beside him. 'I can't wait to see what we're having!'

'Ogden make much yum-yum foods, for to thank Willow!' he said proudly.

Willow grinned. 'Good! I could eat a horse!'

Ogden frowned. 'No horse,' he said, sadly. 'But if Willow wait, Og can go and grab one.'

'No!' Willow said, quickly. 'It's only an expression!' She smiled at him. 'I'll eat whatever you've made me.'

'Ogden make the bestest human foods.' Ogden wrinkled his big chops into a grin, and lightly took hold of the edge of the tablecloth. 'Ta-da!' He removed the tablecloth and revealed the feast below.

Willow looked at her supper. Ogden had made . . .

A delicious starter:

Fresh, juicy blackberries . . . lovingly

sprinkled with chubby maggots.

For the tasty main course:

Gently sautéed mushrooms and black beetles, with a nettle garnish.

And to finish, a sumptuous pudding:

Mud pie. Made with real mud. And real worms.

'Lovely.' Willow gulped. 'Thank you so much, Ogden.'

'We eat the right foods!' Ogden rubbed his gnarly hands together. 'They make us twirl faster, jump higher, dance better!'

Willow removed a maggot from a handful of berries and popped the fruit into her mouth.

'This is delicious, Og!' she smiled, 'You must eat some too.' She handed him a slice of mud pie. 'Would you care for extra worms with that? I couldn't possibly manage all of mine.'

The next morning, Willow had a surprise for Ogden. When he arrived at the tree house, she was reading a newspaper called *The Daily Bagpipe*.

'Look at this!' she thrust the paper under his warty nose. 'There's a dance competition in the village hall. We've got to enter. This is our chance to show everything we've learned together!'

Ogden's mouth turned down at the corners. 'But humans will run away again.'

'Don't give up, dancer!' said Willow. 'We'll disguise you. My aunty has a clothes shop in the village. We'll visit her this evening and she'll help.'

★

'**Psssst!**'

Ogden shook himself awake. The sun was setting behind the snow-capped mountains. He must have fallen asleep on the grassy knoll where Willow had told him to meet her. What was that noise?

'**Pssssst!**'

It was Willow! He suddenly remembered they were going to visit her aunty and his tum felt giggly and nervous again. Willow was wearing a very large moss-green cape with the hood pulled low over her face.

'Quickly, put this on!' she urged, taking off the cape and giving it to him. 'Now if we do meet anyone, they won't see your face.'

'Yes, little Will.' Ogden liked the feeling of the soft, warm velvet on his bald head.

Willow led him down the narrow path through the trees, and skipped over flat stones that crossed a shimmering stream. After a short while they came to a fence with a five-bar gate. Although it was getting quite dark, Ogden could see the village ahead, the warm, orange lights from windows shining out into the night. Willow opened the gate and led Ogden towards some wooden buildings then down a cobbled alleyway and on to a road.

'Are we nearly there yet?' Ogden

whispered. 'When do we have yummy supper?'

'Ssh!' Willow said, pulling his hand. 'This way!'

The air was thick with the smell of oil lamps burning, the light flickering and casting shadows on the street. Ogden looked at each building as they walked; they passed the baker's shop, the cobbler's and the fishmonger's, before finally coming to a small shop with a sign on the front. It said *Fenella's Fashions* in shiny gold letters. In the window were mannequins wearing dazzling clothes with sequins sewn on them.

'Pretty!' purred Ogden.

Willow opened the door and they walked in. 'Aunty Fenella?'

A pair of black lace-up boots appeared

through a hole in the ceiling. The boots were attached to legs in stripy stockings. The legs were attached to a body wearing a blue minidress and the body was attached to a head with a shock of ginger curls on top. Aunty Fenella whizzed down a fireman's pole into the room, her glasses balanced on her nose and her mouth full of dress pins.

'Wotcha!' she said. 'Got your friend with you, then?'

Willow nodded. 'Aunty, this is Ogden.'

Ogden shyly stretched out his gnarly hand. 'Pleased to meet you, Aunty Fenella.'

'Pleased to meet you, Ogden,' said Aunty Fenella through a mouthful of pins, shaking Ogden's hand vigorously . . . so vigorously, that the hood of Ogden's cape suddenly fell away, showing his face.

'*Aargh!*' Aunty Fenella spat the pins out of her mouth in shock. She ran to the fireman's pole and desperately tried to pull herself up into the attic again. 'Run for your lives, we'll all be eaten!' she yelled at Willow, sliding down the pole despite her best efforts. She jumped onto the counter, brandishing her pinking shears at Ogden. 'I'll do for you, I swear it! Stay away, you ogre!'

'Aunty!' said Willow, 'He's my friend. I told you he was . . . different.'

'You didn't tell me he was a man-eating monster!' cried Aunty Fenella.

'He's not!' Willow insisted. 'He promised faithfully never to eat another human being and he's stuck to it. He even saved my life. You're perfectly safe – isn't she, Ogden?'

Ogden nodded so hard he thought his head might fall off. 'Aunty too-too skinny for a proper meal, anyhow.'

'As long as you're sure,' said Fenella nervously. 'I'd heard tell that more and more monsters were coming into these parts. Some poor folk have been eaten!' She pursed her lips at Willow. 'Your days in that tree house are numbered, my girl!'

'Aunty!' Willow cried. 'You promised me I could spend the summer there. Soon it will be autumn and I'll be home with you here in the village and back at school. Anyway, I've got Ogden to protect me now. All the other monsters are frightened of him.'

'You betcha.' Fenella nodded. 'I can see why.' She waggled her pinking shears at Ogden. 'I haven't seen an ogre this close up for a dozen summers. And my, that ogre was a gnarly one. Tall as you, and twice as ugly. And you know what I did to him? I poked him in the bum with my scissors!' She jabbed at Ogden. 'One false move from you, ogre, and you won't sit down for a week!'

'Aunty!' cried Willow.

Ogden held up his hands. 'Og promise no eat Aunty. Aunty make the clothes for to dance!' He smiled a shy smile at Fenella.

'Hmm . . .' Fenella picked up her tape measure and approached Ogden slowly. 'So you're a dancer, eh?' she said. 'Big fella, aren't you?' She held the tape up to him. 'This will have to be a very special suit.'

'But can you make it for him?' asked Willow.

'You betcha!' Aunty Fenella raised an

eyebrow at him. 'So what kind of outfit do you want, Ogden?'

'Sparkles! In the deepest red of cherries!' he said, pointing to a mannequin wearing a dress covered in scarlet sequins.

'Ogden . . . that's a ladies' dress,' said Willow.

'And those feets,' he pointed at some high-heeled shoes.

'Ogden, they're for ladies too! You can't wear them,' said Willow.

Ogden hung his head and a small tear plopped onto the floor. 'Sparkles,' he said, quietly.

'The ogre wants to wear a dress,' said Aunty Fenella, her hand on her hip. 'Well, why not? It would be a good way to disguise him, yes? You betcha. With a big wig and make-up.'

'Good plan, Aunty,' said Ogden, and sniffed.

'But that means I have to be in disguise too,' said Willow. 'As a man!'

'You'll look very handsome with a top hat and a bow tie,' said Aunty Fenella. 'Now let me go in the back and see if I have that dress in his size . . .'

'Don't forget my two left feets,' said Ogden, beaming.

Aunty Fenella looked down at Ogden's huge, green feet with their long, painted glittery nails.

'Jumping juniper berries, two left feet! Forget them? I don't think I ever could,' she said, winking at him. 'Now where did I leave my measuring tape?'

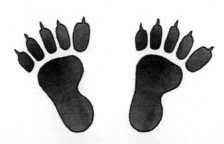

Ogden and Willow practised their dancing extra hard all week. On the morning of the competition, Ogden rose before the sun and crept through the woods to Willow's tree house.

'Wakey-wakey, Willow!' he called softly.

Willow's blonde head appeared through the branches.

'I haven't slept a wink, I'm too nervous!' she whispered back.

They made their way quickly through the woods to the village. Ogden wore the velvet cloak, but no one was up except the baker, baking loaves in his shop. The delicious smell of warm bread wafted into Ogden's nostrils.

'Mmm! Yeasty-dough and pastry cakes!' he said, then sniffed the air again. 'And yum-yum baker too!'

'Ogden!' Willow said, sharply. 'No humans, remember?'

Ogden shook himself. 'No humans. Dance with humans.'

'That's better,' Willow replied. 'Anyway, I don't know how you could think of food, I'm far too nervous.'

Willow knocked on the door of Aunty Fenella's shop with a secret **rat-tat-tat-tat!** A hand appeared around the door and pulled them in.

'Did anyone see you?' Fenella said.

'Not a soul,' replied Willow.

'Then we'll begin our work, yes? You betcha.'

Fenella rolled up her sleeves and pointed to a large chair in the middle of the room. 'Ogden, my friend. Take a seat.'

The makeover began. Fenella shaved Ogden's whiskers and trimmed his ear tufts. Willow powdered his face pink and painted his fingernails pillar-box red.

'Ouch!' Og cried, as Fenella plucked a particularly long nose hair.

'Much better,' Fenella said. 'Ogden, when I'm done with you, you'll be buffed and puffed and as pretty as a daisy.'

Ogden grinned at her. 'A very *big* daisy.'

Willow changed into a black suit, with a sparkling red bow tie. She stuck a ginger moustache on her face and tucked her long hair into a top hat.

'I'm a perfect gentleman!' she said, bowing low. 'Where is my lady?'

Fenella placed a large wig of glossy black curls on Ogden's head. 'No one will guess you are an ogre now,' she said, fixing a glittering tiara in his wig.

'But what about the dress?' said Willow.

'I always save the best till last,' said Fenella. She wheeled out a huge mannequin covered by a dark blue silk cloth. 'Are you ready, Ogden?'

Ogden nodded.

'May you dazzle and sparkle with the best of them!' cried Aunty Fenella, whipping the blue cloth away. There on the mannequin was a beautiful cherry-red dress covered in sequins.

It shimmered in the lamp light, almost seeming to move.

'Wow!' cried Willow.

Ogden rose slowly and reached out to touch the dress. **'Sparkly!'** he whispered.

'And here are your shoes!' said Fenella. 'A gold shoe for your left-left foot, and silver for your right-left foot.'

Ogden put everything on and Fenella wheeled out a long mirror. 'Well, what do you think?'

Ogden stared at his reflection.

'You look incredible!' cried Willow.

Ogden stared some more.

'You're stunning, you betcha,' said Fenella.

Ogden stared the longest stare.

'Ogden? Are you all right?' said Willow.

Suddenly Ogden leaped high into the air and, before Willow or Aunty Fenella

could do anything to stop him, he was swooping and swirling around the shop as fast as his two left feet would let him.

'**Weeeeeeeeeeeeeeeeee!**' he cried as he swooshed past Aunty Fenella, spinning her like a top.

'**Woooooooooooooo!**' he hollered, as he grabbed Willow and whirled her around like a tornado.

'**Whaaaaaaaaaaaaaaaaaa!**' yelled Fenella and Willow, as they struggled to keep up, flying around the shop in a rainbow of sequins and sparkles.

Finally Willow grabbed the fireman's pole and slowed herself to a stop. 'It's time to go!'

'Make sure you come back winners, yes?' said Fenella, panting.

'You betcha!' said Ogden, heading for the door.

Willow led the way through the village and Ogden trotted neatly behind on his glittery heels. At the fishmonger's, the shop owner was setting out his wares.

'Good morning!' he called.

'Good morning!' growled Willow in her gravelliest voice.

They passed the cobbler's shop, which was opening for business. The cobbler, his wife and their three fat babies waved at them from the window.

'Good day to you!' boomed Willow.

The baker was standing against his doorway in the morning sun.

'Where might you fine folk be going?' he said.

'We're the best dancers in the land and

we're off to the competition,' said Willow proudly.

'Good luck to you then,' said the baker. 'And you, lady,' he looked at Ogden closely, 'are the fairest maid I've seen for many a day. Permit me to kiss your hand?'

Ogden gulped. Before he could say anything, the baker had taken his gnarly hand and planted a squelchy kiss on it.

'But wait!' The baker disappeared inside his shop and reappeared a second later. 'Please take this cake. It is the finest cake I've made today, for the finest lady in this village.'

Ogden eyed the cake and his tum rumbled loudly. He grabbed it and ate it in a single gulp.

The baker's jaw dropped. 'I like a woman with a good appetite!'

Ogden burped loudly – 'Oops!' – and quickly covered his mouth with his hand.

Willow hurried him away to the doors of the village hall. She checked her ginger moustache, straightened her hat and squeezed Ogden's arm.

'This is it, Og – let's knock 'em dead!'

Ogden and Willow walked into the hall. Ogden looked around him and gasped. The room was spinning with colour. There were dozens of dancers in shimmering costumes, the crystals and sequins on their clothes casting little rainbows on the walls as they pirouetted across the floor. Above them, a painted banner hung from the rafters, with words in big, red letters. Willow read it out: 'Dancing Competition Heats.'

Ogden furrowed his brow. 'Why it heats, little Will? We get hot?'

Willow giggled. 'No, it means that

the winners from today go through to the Grand Final. If we win, we'll have to dance again.'

'I want to dance again,' said Ogden.

They walked up to a little man sitting at a table. He had pursed lips and a monocle and kept tapping his pen on the list in front of him.

'Name?' he said.

'Willow,' said Willow. Ogden gave her a sharp nudge in the ribs.

'Willow . . . is the name of my lovely dance partner here!' said Willow quickly. 'And my name is Ogden.'

'Hmmm . . . Yes, I have you on my list,' the little man snapped. 'Here are your numbers.' He handed Willow two pieces of paper with a large number printed on each one. 'You can warm up on the floor, and then you'll be called for the first dance. Good luck.'

Willow turned to pin one of the numbers on Ogden's dress.

'We're number thirteen! Lucky for some!' she whispered. 'Now pin mine on the back of my jacket, will you?'

The band was playing a gentle waltz – one-two-three! One-two-three!

'Time for warm up.' Willow grabbed Ogden's hand. 'Just like we do in the forest.'

Odgen licked his lips nervously, and they began to move around the floor, slowly at first. They passed a dashing couple who looked as if they were floating on air. The lady was wearing a dress made of yellow feathers.

'Lady look like a canary!' giggled Ogden.

Then there was a stunning pair of dancers both dressed in shiny emerald silk.

'Them green, like ogres!' Ogden winked at Willow.

'Try to concentrate, Ogden!' hissed Willow.

At that moment the music stopped and the little man tapped his pen on the microphone.

'Clear the floor please, clear the floor!'

Everyone did.

'Our first dance is the Waltz,' said the little man. 'At the end, I will read out the numbers of the contestants who will proceed to the next dance. The judges' decision is final!'

Ogden looked up at the stage where the judges were sitting behind a table. There were three of them: a lady with blonde hair and diamond earrings, a tall, thin man

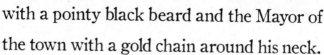

with a pointy black beard and the Mayor of the town with a gold chain around his neck.

'Don't forget to smile, Og,' Willow whispered to Ogden. 'Especially at the Mayor!'

'I ate Mayor once,' said Ogden thoughtfully. 'Not that one, though.'

Suddenly the band started to play and the dancers took to the floor.

'This is it!' said Willow. Ogden swallowed, and smiled his sweetest smile.

They waltzed around the floor, concentrating hard on getting all the steps right. All was going well, until couple number seven slipped and fell, and others crashed into them with a *wallop!*

'Uh oh, pile-up!' said Ogden, as Willow guided him round the unlucky heap of dancers. Ogden's dress billowed out behind

him and he grinned at the judges happily.

The music ended and all the remaining couples came to a halt. The little man came to the microphone again.

'The judges have decided who will proceed to the tango.'

Willow held Ogden's hand tightly.

'Couple numbers one, two, four, five, eight, ten and twelve,' the man paused and looked up from his list. 'And couple numbers thirteen, fourteen and sixteen. That is all.'

'We did it, Og!' said Willow, trying not to jump up and down with excitement.

'We did?' Ogden could hardly believe it. 'We can dance again?' There was no time to think as the band started to play a dramatic tango and the couples took to the floor for a second time. Willow put on her most serious face, grabbed Ogden's hand and immediately swung him into a low swoon in front of the judges. His wig wobbled, but luckily it didn't fall off.

'Oooh!' said the audience, and clapped their hands.

The tango was fast and furious and everything was a blur to Ogden as Willow swept him round again and again, just as they had practised. Eventually the music stopped and the couples left the floor, trying not to pant too hard.

'This'll be a tricky one, Og,' said Willow. 'They'll eliminate far more couples than last time. Cross your fingers for number thirteen.'

The judges huddled together, and all the couples shifted nervously in their seats. At last the little man came to the microphone.

'It's been a difficult decision,' he said, gravely. 'I will now read out the numbers.'

Ogden crossed all his fingers and his sparkly toes too, and waited.

Ogden was so nervous he wanted to scratch his head, but decided it wasn't very ladylike. And rather difficult with his big wig and crossed fingers.

The little man cleared his throat. 'Going through to the next round are . . . couples one, two, five and eight. Congratulations!'

'Oh, Og!' Willow's face crumpled.

'And,' the man continued, '. . . lucky number thirteen!' Willow let out a high-pitched squeal, then quickly tried to cover it up with a coughing fit.

'Stand up straight, dancer!' said Ogden, thumping her on the back. 'Time for **cha-cha!**' He led the way to the dance floor. 'Ogden's favourite!'

Willow whispered in his ear. 'We need to do our absolute best and beat all these other dancers. Are you ready?' Ogden nodded his head so much his wig nearly fell off. Willow stood on her tiptoes and straightened his tiara. 'Then let's show 'em how it's done!'

The familiar beat of the **cha-cha** made Ogden's toes start to tap. He shut his eyes, listened to the music and pretended he was in the clearing in the wood by the tree house. What a long way he had come in a few weeks! He opened his eyes and Willow whizzed him past the judges in a thrilling **Whooooosh!** of colour.

'**Aaaaaaaah!**' gasped the audience.

Ogden and Willow pranced around the dance floor, Ogden's glittering two left feet as quick and dazzling as fireworks. As the music ended, Ogden lifted one arm in a beautiful arc, and swished his left-left foot up behind his head and held it high in the air in a stunning feat of balance.

'Bravo!' said the audience.

Suddenly, a stray yellow feather from a dancer's dress wafted under Willow's nose. '**A-a-a-a . . . tish-ooooo!**' she sneezed. Ogden watched in horror as Willow's ginger moustache flew through the air and landed on the tip of his nose.

'**Oooooooooh!**' cried the audience.

Ogden darted out his long tongue and gobbled up the moustache.

'**Ewwwww!**' went the audience.

The little man took off his monocle and rubbed it with a handkerchief. 'Er . . . thank you, dancers. There will now be a short break while the judges make their decision,' he said.

Willow and Ogden quickly sat down at the back of the hall.

'I'm so sorry!' said Willow out of the corner of her mouth. 'I couldn't stop myself from sneezing. I wish I wasn't allergic to feathers. Now everyone will know I'm a girl!'

'Your ginger moustache did not taste of ginger,' said Ogden, thoughtfully.

'I hope we're not disqualified,' said Willow. 'Perhaps no one noticed what happened?'

'Oh no, everyone see it,' said Ogden. 'But maybe they thinks you is a little boy who can't grow a real moustache?'

There was a drum roll.

'It is now time to announce the winners who will go through to the Grand Final!' said the little man from the stage. Ogden and Willow held their breath.

'The winners are . . . couple number . . . eight!'

The canary woman screamed and jumped up in the air in a flurry of yellow feathers. Her partner caught her and they cha-cha-ed across the dance floor and hugged the judges.

Willow looked at Ogden. 'I can't believe it. It's so unfair. We deserved – *you* deserved to win.'

'Don't worry, little Willow,' said Ogden. 'Ogres not supposed to win dancing competitions. Ogden had whole heap of fun with the sparkles anyway.'

A tear ran down Willow's cheek.

'Don't cry, little Will,' said Ogden. 'Boys don't cry. Even ones with fake moustaches.'

'Ahem!' It was the Mayor, standing on the stage with his hands on his hips. 'Can couple thirteen come to the stage, please?'

'Oh goodness! That's us!' said Willow. She took Ogden's hand and they walked onto the stage.

The Mayor looked them up and down.

'Something fishy is going on here. We judges do not like to be deceived!' The Mayor whipped off Willow's top hat and long blonde hair tumbled on to her shoulders. 'I knew it!' he cried. 'You are quite plainly a girl and not a man at all! Why on earth did you wear a disguise?'

'Um . . .' said Willow.

'Did you think that *two ladies* could not dance together?' said the Mayor.

'Er . . .' said Willow.

'Luckily for you we think that is a very old-fashioned way to do things. Your dancing was so good that we have decided to award you two ladies the "Wildcard" entry to the Grand Final! You too will dance for the honour of this village!'

The crowd let out an almighty cheer! Ogden scooped Willow up into his arms and spun her round.

'Jumping juniper berries! We made it!' cried Willow.

'We dance again! With sparkles and rainbow colours!' said Ogden.

The band struck up a happy tune and a photographer from *The Daily Bagpipe* took a picture of the winning couples.

Willow and Ogden hurried back to Fenella's shop. They knocked on the door with a special **rat-tat-tat-tat!** Fenella let them in.

'We did it, Aunty! We did it!' said Willow.

'What?' said Fenella. 'You're in the Grand Final?'

'They give us a "Wildcard". Because we're wild . . . **grrrrr!**' said Ogden, growling.

'You betcha!' said Aunt Fenella, throwing her arms around them both and hugging them tightly. 'Now let's celebrate properly with my elderflower champagne! Only the best for you, Ogden my friend!'

The celebration lasted long into the night. Willow was allowed a tiny sip of elderflower champagne, although she was a bit too young and the bubbles went up her nose. Ogden drank it with big gulps, and had a huge attack of the burps. Fenella laughed at their tales of the competition, especially the part when Willow sneezed her moustache off and Ogden ate it.

Finally, the village clock chimed midnight.

'Look at that ogre!' said Fenella, trying not to hiccup. 'He's fast asleep!'

Ogden was snoring loudly, still wearing his dress of deepest red sequins. All of his make-up had rubbed off, his wig had gone and he looked very peculiar lying on the counter. Mmm . . . Ogden was dreaming of the sparkles.

'**Wakey-wakey!**' called Willow. 'It's way past our bedtimes.'

Ogden woke up, a little wobbly from sleep and champagne. He took off his dress, wrapped his trusty pink feather boa around his neck and pulled the moss-green cloak over his shoulders. He and Willow said their goodbyes to Aunty Fenella and stepped out into the street.

'How my legs ache! I don't think I can stay awake,' said Willow.

Ogden scooped her up into his strong arms.

'No worry, little Will. Home you go for sleepy wink-winks,' he said.

Ogden carried the slumbering Willow through the village, past the fishmonger's, the cobbler's and the baker's shops, all in darkness. In the distance, he could see lights in the village hall and hear the faint sounds of music. The people there were still having a party after the competition. Ogden thought about them there, a whole room full of tasty humans. The dancing and the champagne burps had made him hungry – very hungry – and his tum groaned because it was so empty.

But he shook his head.

'No eat humans anymore,' he murmured to himself. He looked down at the sleeping Willow in his arms. 'Ogden promised.'

He trundled towards the forest. 'And we need our sleeps. Get strength for Grand Final.'

★

Willow was having a lovely dream about making a giant snowman out of vanilla ice cream, with cherries for eyes and a raspberry nose.

'Ra-tat-TAT! TAT!'

She woke up with a start and hurried to the hatch in the tree house.

'Ra-tat-TAT! TAT!'

'I'm coming as fast as my dancer's legs will carry me!' She opened the hatch and looked down at a red-faced Aunty Fenella on the ladder below. 'What time is it?' said Willow, rubbing her eyes. 'I'm still sleepy.'

'Thank heavens you're not hurt!' said Fenella, clambering into the tree house.

'Not hurt?' said Willow. 'My legs are a bit achy, but I suppose you'd expect that with all the dancing I did yesterday.'

Fenella took hold of Willow's shoulders. 'Have you seen the picture in the newspaper?'

'Ooh! Are we in it?' said Willow excitedly.

Fenella pursed her lips. 'Ogden is.'

'Oh, goody!' said Willow. 'He'll be so excited.'

'I don't think so,' said Aunty Fenella, looking very serious. 'Here, look.'

Willow took the newspaper. The headline read:

OGRE STEALS TRIPLETS!

Underneath was a blurred photograph of Ogden running away with something in his arms. Willow blinked. 'Am I still dreaming?'

Aunty Fenella shook her head sadly. 'I wish this was just a bad dream, but it's true.' She pored over the newspaper. 'It says here that Ogden crept into the cobbler's house last night and stole the three babies.'

Willow blinked again. 'Ogden wouldn't do a thing like that!'

'Oh, Willow, it breaks my heart to think it, but look!' Fenella tapped the photograph of Ogden with a long, purple fingernail.

'I won't believe it!' Willow cried. 'He said he never ever ate children, even when he was still eating humans.' Before she could help it, a tear ran down her cheek.

'This is very serious, Willow,' said Fenella gently. 'Ogden is a monster, after all, he can't help how he's made. He's an ogre, and ogres eat people. It was only a matter of time before he slipped up.

Leopards don't change their spots.'

'He's not a monster or a leopard, he's my friend!' shouted Willow.

'I'm so sorry, Willow,' said Fenella, 'but when I saw this picture, I had to go and tell the Mayor that I knew who the ogre was.'

'You betrayed Ogden?' said Willow. 'Aunty, how could you?'

'I had to!' Fenella said. 'Those poor babies! And what about you? If he's turned bad again, he'll gobble you up!'

'He'd never hurt me!' Willow cried.

'**Ra-tat-TAT! TAT!**'

Fenella jumped into the air in fright.

'Who is it?' called Willow.

'Let me in!' boomed a loud voice.

'Aaargh! It's the ogre!' cried Fenella. 'Come to eat us!'

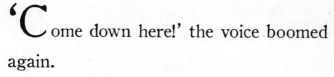

'Come down here!' the voice boomed again.

'That's not Ogden,' said Willow and opened the hatch. There on the ladder stood the Mayor. In the clearing a crowd was gathering. Some of villagers were carrying pitchforks and large sticks.

'I'm in my pyjamas!' Willow said.

'I don't care if you're in your birthday suit!' replied the Mayor. 'Come and face the music! You too, Fenella.'

Willow and her aunty did as they were told and climbed down.

93

'Don't delay, little girl,' said the Mayor to Willow. 'Tell us where the ogre is.'

'Kill the monster! Kill the vicious child-snatcher!' shouted the crowd.

'No!' cried Willow. 'You mustn't hurt him, he's done nothing wrong!'

The cobbler and his wife were pushed to the front of the crowd. They looked hopefully at Willow with teary eyes.

'Please, missy, tell us where that monster has taken our children,' said the cobbler.

'My three pretty babes!' cried the cobbler's wife, sobbing into her hands.

'Ogden hasn't taken them,' Willow said. 'He made a promise!'

The crowd jeered and waved their sticks.

'Willow,' said Fenella. 'You must take

us to his cave. Then we can talk to him. We can find out the truth.'

'All right,' said Willow, 'But only you, Mr Mayor, the cobbler and his wife.'

The crowd grumbled, but the Mayor talked to them quietly and they left to return to the village. Willow stuck her chin in the air and led Fenella, the Mayor, the cobbler and his wife through the woods into the deepest, darkest part of the forest. Willow hoped that the others couldn't see that she was shaking as she marched along. Ogden would never take the babies! But who had? And what would the Mayor do to Ogden when they found him?

After many twists and turns, they finally approached Ogden's cave.

'Stay here!' commanded Willow. 'I'll speak to him first and bring him out.'

'What if he eats you?' said Fenella.

'This is most irregular,' said the Mayor.

'My babies!' cried the cobbler's wife.

Willow took a deep breath and went inside the cave. It was very dark. As she went farther and farther in, the hairs on the back of her neck began to tickle. What if everyone was right? What if Ogden had turned bad? What if he had taken the triplets? Would he eat her too, here in this cave?

She took a few steps and nearly tripped over Ogden's feather boa. She picked it up.

'No!' she whispered, angry with herself. 'How could I doubt him? He'd never break his promise to me!'

She shook herself, and slowly walked farther into the darkness.

'Ogden!' she whispered.

Then she could hear it: a soft murmur coming from the back of the cave. She moved towards the sound.

'Sparkles . . . Cha-cha-cha! Watch the ogre dance!'

Ogden was talking in his sleep!

Willow tiptoed up to him and gently tapped him on the shoulder.

'Ugh?' snorted Ogden. He blinked his eyes. 'Little Will? What bring you here? Something wrong?'

Before she could stop herself, Willow began to cry.

'Poor weeping Willow!' said Ogden, putting his big arm round her. 'Don't sob with the leaky tears!'

'It's awful!' said Willow. 'Everyone thinks that you've eaten the cobbler's triplets!'

'Sillies!' Ogden giggled. 'Ogden no eat humans anymore. Not since the dancing.' He took the feather boa from Willow and wrapped it about his neck.

'There's a photo of you, running away carrying something,' said Willow.

Ogden shook his head. 'I carry you home, for sleepy wink-winks.'

'I knew it!' said Willow. 'Come outside and talk to everyone, won't you?'

'Maybe Og can help find them?' said Ogden. 'Babes can go missing. Them is so very wriggly.'

Willow ran to the mouth of the cave.

'He's coming out!'

She stepped into the fresh air, blinking in the bright light and turned to Ogden. 'Don't worry, Og, they'll believe you.'

Ogden walked out of the cave.

'Now!' shouted the Mayor. A huge net fell from the sky, covering Ogden.

'**Wheeeeeeeee!**' a whistle blew and the crowd of villagers appeared, holding down the edge of the net so that Ogden could not escape.

'No!' cried Willow, running up to the net.

'**Rooooooaaaaaaaaaaaarrrrrr!**' said Ogden, trying to break free. 'Why did you trick Ogden, little Will?' he wailed.

'I didn't!' Willow said. 'Oh, Ogden, please believe me!'

Some of the crowd poked and hit Ogden with their sticks, to stop him from trying to escape.

'Willow . . . help Ogden!' he sobbed, a large tear rolling down his cheek.

'Get off him, you fiends!' shouted Willow.

The crowd surged round Ogden, wrapping him with ropes and chains.

'Stop hurting him!' Willow ran into the middle of all the people, trying to reach Ogden. In the chaos, she was pushed to the ground, beneath the stomping feet of the crowd.

'Willow!' gasped Fenella. She turned to the Mayor. 'They're going to crush her!'

'All cease!' shouted the Mayor. 'Step away from the monster,' he instructed the mob. As the crowd parted, Ogden tried to reach for Willow, but he was caught fast in the net with chains tied around his middle.

'Little Will!' he croaked. 'Og so sad if you be squashed and squished!'

'See!' said Willow, picking herself up off the ground. 'Does that sound like a blood-thirsty baby-eater to you? Search his cave, there's nothing there!' said Willow.

Just at that moment, two men ran out of the cave entrance.

'She's right. There's no sign of the children,' one of the men said.

'There!' said Willow, 'He's innocent!'

'He may have already gobbled them up! He's an ogre and he can't be trusted,' said the Mayor firmly. 'We have absolute proof he took the babies and he'll be taken to jail until we get the truth!'

With that, the Mayor marched the crowd and Ogden off through the forest towards the village.

'Don't lose hope, Ogden!' Willow shouted after him. 'We'll get to the bottom of this, I promise you!' She turned to Fenella, her cheeks flaming red. 'They've got proof that Ogden took the babies? What proof?'

At the jail, Ogden was thrown into a cell by two burly guards.

'Not so fierce now, are you?' said the tallest burly guard.

'Ha! What kind of ogre wears a pink feather boa?' said the smallest burly guard.

'Willow say it suit Ogden,' said Ogden proudly.

The guards left. Ogden sat on a wooden bed and looked around the cell. It was very bare, with pebbles on the floor and stone walls. Through the bars he could see a table and chair in the corner of the room.

There was a window high above the bed, but it was far too tiny to squeeze through.

'Ogden stuck,' he said to himself.

'That's right,' said the Mayor, walking in. 'Now tell us where you've hidden the babies. Or did you eat them?'

'Don't eat humans anymore,' said Ogden. 'And never eat child-humans. Them too-too skinny and wiggly.'

'Don't deny it!' said the Mayor, walking up to the cell bars. 'You're an ogre, and ogres eat people. Besides, we have proof. There are footprints in the mud beneath the babies' bedroom window. Huge footprints.'

Ogden looked down at his feet. 'Huge feets,' he nodded. 'But Ogden didn't take the babes.'

The Mayor pointed to his pocket watch. 'You have until midnight, ogre. If you don't tell us what you have done with the triplets, you'll be for the chop.' He left the room, slamming the door behind him.

Ogden scratched his head. Had he been into the cobbler's garden? No, he hadn't. How had his footprints got there? His head felt befuddled with it all.

The tallest burly guard walked into the room, keys clinking on his belt. Behind him was Willow.

'Ogden!' She ran to him.

'Little Will!' Ogden hugged her through the bars.

'Oi!' said the guard. 'Get your hands off 'er! Stay away from him, miss, he'll bite your head off!' he said to Willow.

Willow's face flushed red with anger. 'No he won't! Can't you get that into your thick brain?!' she said.

Ogden giggled.

'Aren't you the feisty one?' said the tallest burly guard. 'Five minutes is all you got, then you're out of here.' He slumped on a chair in the corner.

Willow looked at Ogden. 'Are you hurt?'

'Them teeny sticks and stones not enough to break my bones!' he winked at her.

'Your feather boa – it's practically bare,' Willow said, looking at it hanging round Ogden's neck. 'We'll get you out of here, don't worry!'

'Them thinks I sneaky-sneaked up to the babes' window. Them sees my feets in the mud,' Ogden said.

'Footprints?' asked Willow. 'Impossible! They must belong to someone else.'

'Too huge for humans,' said Ogden sadly. 'Ogre-size.'

'I'll go and look myself,' said Willow.

'Take care,' said Ogden. 'Who knows what lurks in Cobblerman's garden?'

A grunt came from the guard in the corner. He had fallen asleep and was snoring loudly.

'Some guard he is,' said Willow. 'Snoozing away with the keys on his belt like that.'

Willow and Ogden looked at each other. The same idea came into both of their heads at once. 'Now's our chance!' said Willow.

'Be carefully-careful, little Will!' said Ogden.

Willow crept across the room. The guard's chest rose and fell with each deep snore. She got closer and closer until she could almost reach the keys. She stretched out her hand—

'Snufla flort!' The guard gave a little snort in his sleep.

Willow sprang back and Ogden giggled nervously into his hands. Shaking, Willow reached forward again and gently took the bunch of keys. Very carefully she started to unclip them from the tallest burly guard's belt—

'**Stop!**' A voice cried out from the doorway.

Willow jumped with fright and the keys flew up into the air. Ogden reached out a long arm and deftly caught them!

'Give the keys to me!' The voice belonged to the smallest burly guard.

'Quick, unlock the door, Ogden!' cried Willow. She bent double and ran at the smallest burly guard with all her might, tackling him to the ground. Ogden tried the first key in the lock. It didn't fit.

'What's going on?' said the tallest burly guard, waking up.

Ogden tried the second key. It did not fit.

''E's got the keys!' yelled the smallest burly guard from the floor.

'Not so fast!' said the tallest burly guard and rushed towards Ogden. Ogden snatched the keys out of the lock and backed away into his cell.

'You give 'em back!' said the smallest burly guard. He scrambled to his feet and held Willow by her ear. 'If you don't, the little girl gets it!' He gave her ear a sharp tug, making her cry out.

'Don't you hurt my Willow!' cried

Ogden, rushing to the bars and thrusting the keys at the man. 'Let her go, you weany-meany Guardman!'

'Ogden, no!' said Willow.

The smallest burly guard snatched the keys from Ogden. He turned to his friend. 'Pah! You can't be trusted. These keys will be kept in plain sight from now on.' He slapped the keys down on the table, out of reach. 'And as for you, you little minx,' he said to Willow, 'You're banished from the jail!' With that he pulled her out of the room by her ear.

'I'll be back, Ogden!' cried Willow from outside.

'Oh, no you won't!' the tallest burly guard snarled, and followed them out of the room, his head bowed.

Ogden sat down on the bed and sighed a

big sigh. How close he'd been to escaping! He kicked some pebbles across the floor and watched as the last strips of sunlight disappeared from his cell. He tried to think some nice thoughts, but none would come. Soon it would be midnight and the Mayor would be back. How could he confess to something he hadn't done? And just how had his footprints ended up in the cobbler's garden?

'Aunty! Let me in!'

Willow banged on the door of Fenella's Fashions. She had run all the way from the jail and was quite out of breath. The door opened. A hand grabbed Willow and pulled her into the shop. Fenella locked the door and put the chain on.

'I need to borrow one of your measuring tapes and a pencil and paper,' said Willow.

'Whatever for?' said Fenella.

'I'm going to the cobbler's house,' said Willow. 'The Mayor said that the footprints in the mud were so big that they must be Ogden's, but I'm going to prove he's wrong.'

'Then I'm coming too,' said Fenella. 'I'm the only one who knows Ogden's measurements – I made his shoes!'

Willow nodded. 'It could be dangerous. If I'm right, whoever stole the babies is still out there.'

They ran all the way to the cobbler's house and snuck into the garden. Willow peeped around a bush. 'Coast is clear!' They crept across the lawn towards the house until they reached the mud by the wall. The ground was a mushy mess, but just below the triplets' window there was a patch of smooth mud . . . with two huge footprints.

'There they are!' said Fenella. 'Quick sticks, night time's not far off. Let's copy them on to the paper before its gets too dark to see.'

Willow bent down and traced the two footprints.

'They are big,' said Fenella, looking over Willow's shoulder.

'But they can't be Ogden's!' said Willow furiously. She held the tape measure up to the prints.

Fenella checked the measurements in her notebook. 'Oh, Willow. They're exactly the same size.'

Willow grabbed the book to read it herself. 'I won't believe it!' She dissolved into tears.

'You've done your best for him,' said Fenella. 'Let's get you home for a strong cup of blackberry tea.' She put her arms around Willow and they both walked slowly and miserably back to the shop.

Ogden was counting dancing sheep in his head and trying to get to sleep. The cell was very dark. The only light came from outside the window as the moon rose in the night sky. Ogden's tum rumbled. He hadn't eaten anything since yesterday, and that seemed like a very long time ago. He wondered if the Mayor would be coming back soon. He wondered where the babies were and hoped Willow was safe.

As he lay thinking all these thoughts, there was a rustling outside the window. Was somebody there? He stood on his bed and tried to peer out.

The moon had moved behind a cloud. In the gloom he could see a shape moving through the trees. Willow? He was about to call out when suddenly two other shapes appeared. They moved closer and a strange smell filled Ogden's nostrils. The cloud shifted and the moon shone bright onto the figures below.

It was the **Fleshfeasting Fluffy Grocklers!**

They were each carrying a picnic basket in their claws and cackling to one another.

'Scrumptious! Scrumptious! Catchy humans!' said the largest Fluffy Grockler.

'Trap 'em in the village hall!' said the medium Fluffy Grockler.

'Oodles of humans for us to munch on!' said the littlest Fluffy Grockler.

Ogden blinked. Could he believe his ears? The Grocklers were planning to trap the villagers in the hall? He peeped further over the windowsill.

One of the Fluffy Grocklers reached inside its basket. 'Cooky-choo, little babe! You babes will help us catch 'em scrumptious humans!'

A baby popped out of the basket. Ogden gasped. The Grocklers had the triplets! From the sounds of it, the Grocklers were going to use the babies to lure the rest of the humans, to trap them!

Ogden thought the hardest thoughts he'd ever thought. How could he save the babies? How could he warn the villagers?

Whatever he did, he'd have to get out of jail first. The guards wouldn't believe him. He'd have to act, and act fast. The moon's rays streamed through the tiny window, making something on the table glint.

The keys!

Ogden pressed himself tight up to the bars and stretched his arm out as far as it would go, but it was useless. The keys were completely out of reach.

'You must eat something,' said Auntie Fenella, holding out a slice of blueberry pie to Willow.

'I couldn't eat a thing,' she said.

'It's almost midnight,' Fenella said. 'The people will be meeting in the village hall to decide what to do with Ogden.' She filled Willow's teacup.

'I still can't believe it,' said Willow, 'I thought he'd changed. All those happy times we spent together dancing, giggling . . . trying on our costumes.'

'It was lots of fun,' agreed Fenella. 'I've never had to make such a large dress before. And those shoes! Not often you have to make a pair of shoes for someone with two left feet!'

Willow looked at Fenella. She dropped her cup of tea.

'Willow! What's wrong?' said Fenella.

'Oh, I've been so stupid!' cried Willow, holding up the drawing of the footprints. 'What do you see?'

Fenella looked at the drawing closely. 'Two feet.'

'Yes, but what *kind* of feet?' said Willow impatiently.

'Big ones. A big left one and a big right one,' said Fenella. Suddenly her mouth dropped open. 'Oh!' she gasped.

'Exactly!' said Willow. 'These can't belong to Ogden, he has two left feet! Two *left* feet!'

Ogden stared out of the window. It was hopeless; there was nothing he could do to get the keys. The breeze rustled the leaves of the trees, whispering secrets into the night. The pink feather boa around his neck blew into his face and tickled his nose. He took it off and looked at it. He'd never need it again, there would be no more dancing now.

The keys glistened in the moonlight,

temptingly near, but not close enough. If only he had something to get hold of them with!

Suddenly, he realised he did. The pink feather boa!

Quickly, he tied a pebble to one end of the boa to weigh it down, and made a large loop at the same end. Leaning through the bars he threw the boa towards the table like a lasso.

It missed.

He pulled it in and tried a second time. This time the loop landed over the keys. He pulled the boa gently and the loop closed around the keys – it was working!

'Gently-gentle, shiny keys.' Ogden dragged the keys across the table and they fell to the floor with a clinking sound.

'Come to Ogden!' He quickly tugged on

the boa and the keys came through the bars of his cell and stopped at his feet!

The fourth key he tried fitted and the lock opened easily.

'Now we go, oh-so quietly.' He tiptoed across the room and opened the door a crack. The tallest burly guard was sleeping at the desk in the next room. Ogden crept past him, grabbed the rope and the net that the villagers had used to catch him, and put them in a large sack.

'You be needing these.' He winked at the sleeping jailer, placed the keys on the desk and silently sidled out of the front door. He was free!

In the distance, the lights were on at the village hall. Ogden ran, flitting through the shadows.

He hoped he wasn't going to be too late.

Ogden scrambled up on to the roof of the village hall, his sack over his shoulder, like Father Christmas. He crawled across the tiles and opened a trapdoor. Inside the room, there was a long beam of wood across the ceiling, wide enough for him to stand on. A perfect place to hide! He quietly lowered himself onto the beam, and crouched out of sight. Below, the Mayor was talking to the villagers.

'We have searched all day for the babes,' said the Mayor. 'Time is up. The ogre will pay the price!'

The crowd roared and shook their fists in the air.

'No he won't!'

Ogden heard a familiar voice shouting from the door. 'Little Will!' he whispered to himself, excited and nervous.

Willow walked into the hall with her chin held high, followed by Fenella. 'I have proof that Ogden didn't take the triplets,' Willow said. 'We went to the scene of the crime and made this drawing.' She held a piece of paper in the air.

Ogden squinted, and tried to see.

The Mayor strode up to Willow, and looked closely at the drawing.

'The footprints *are* exactly the same size as Ogden's feet. I've measured them,' said Fenella.

'Well?' said the Mayor.

'They're not Ogden's footprints,' said Fenella.

'Why not?' said the Mayor, frowning.

'Because,' said Willow, 'Ogden has two *left* feet.'

'Two left feet?' said the Mayor, 'I've never heard of such a thing!'

'It's true!' said Willow. 'Bring him here and you will see for yourselves.'

'Bring the ogre!' shouted the crowd. 'Check his feet!'

Ogden smiled a crinkly smile. He gripped the beam and was about to jump down, when—

'**Whaaaaaa!**' There was a noise from outside.

'**Whaaaaaaaaa!**' Another noise!

'**Whaaaaaaaaaaaaaaaaa!**' And again!

Everyone ran to the windows and Ogden

ran along the beam to see, too. There, outside on the grass, were three baskets. As he watched, three babies climbed out of the baskets and began to wriggle towards the doorway.

'Jumping juniper berries!' said Willow.

'It's the triplets!' shouted the Mayor.

'My babies!' cried the cobbler's wife and fainted on the spot.

The crowd surged towards the door.

'No!' Ogden shouted at the top of his voice.

Everyone stopped and looked up.

'**Ogden!**' shouted Willow.

'You betcha!' said Fenella.

'The ogre!' cried the Mayor and fainted on the spot too, just next to the cobbler's wife.

'Don't open door!' Ogden shouted down to the crowd. **'A trap! A trap!'**

But it was too late, the door had been opened. A loud screech came through the trees and the Fleshfeasting Fluffy Grocklers lollopped inside, gnashing their horrible teeth. 'Run for your lives!' shouted the crowd, but the Grocklers were already circling them, like lions around a herd of buffalo.

'Tango time!'

Without a pause, Ogden jumped down and landed on top of the littlest Grockler with a resounding crunch. It lay dazed on the floor, spluttering. Ogden sprang to his feet and threw a rope from his bag to the stunned crowd.

'Tie danger-monster!' he said to them. They quickly did as they were told.

Ogden raised himself up to his full height and faced the two other Fluffy Grocklers.

'**Rooooaaaaaaarrrrrrrr!**' he cried.

'**Screeeeeeeeaaaaaaaaaaaaaaaach!**' the Grocklers screamed and dashed at Ogden from either side. Just before they reached him, Ogden pirouetted on his two left feet, leaped gracefully in the air and grabbed the beam above.

'Boooof!' The Grocklers crashed into one another and lay sprawling on the floor. Ogden quickly got the net out of his sack and before the medium Grockler could fully recover, threw the net down upon it. 'Hold it fast!' he shouted to the crowd below. The people pinned the net down so the Grockler could not escape.

'**Ogden! Help!**'

There was a cry from the far end of the room. Ogden turned on the beam, just in time to see Willow being picked up and carried away by the largest Grockler. The crowd gasped. Willow wriggled and kicked as much as she could, but the Grockler held her tightly and ran for the door.

Ogden ran along the beam towards them. He reached into the sack but there was nothing left, except his pink feather boa. Nearly all the feathers were gone now. 'Willow! Catch!' He threw the boa down to her. She caught it and looked up at him, puzzled. Then her nose began to twitch . . .

'**Aaaaaaaa-tish-ooo!**' Willow sneezed so hard that she flew out of the largest Grockler's arms!

Ogden jumped from the beam, throwing the sack over the Grockler's head.

133

Blindly, it tried to run, but as it dashed past Ogden, he stuck out his left-left foot and sent it crashing to the ground. At once the crowd leaped upon it so it could not escape.

'What . . . what is happening?' the Mayor woke up and looked around him.

'Don't worry, Mr Mayorman,' said Ogden, standing guard over the pile of Grocklers. 'All danger-monsters caught now. And them has muddy feets!' He pointed at the largest Grockler's feet. 'Huge ones!'

'Where are my triplets?' said the cobbler's wife, waking up too.

'Safe and sound,' said Fenella, walking into the hall with three large babies in her arms.

'Ogden saved the day!' said Willow to the Mayor.

'In spite of the fact that no one believed in him.' She gave Ogden a big hug. 'Great dance moves, Og.'

Ogden blushed as red as a cherry-red dress. 'Ogden have good teacher.'

The cobbler walked up to Ogden. 'Thank you, ogre. What can I ever do to repay you?'

'Yes,' said the Mayor. 'We owe you a big apology. What can we do to make amends?'

Ogden scratched his head and turned even more red. 'You be needing someone to look after Grocklers in jail. Them Guardmans are sillies. I be new Guard Ogre for you if you wants.'

'You're hired!' said the Mayor. 'But you must want something else?'

'Maybe Mr Cobblerman make new shoes for my two left feets? With purple shinies and silver-gold sparkles? For to dance with?' Ogden said shyly.

'With pleasure, ogre,' said the cobbler.

'You're going to need them. We've got some serious practising to do if we want to win the Grand Final, dancer!' said Willow.

'An ogre with two left feet, dancing?' laughed the Mayor. 'I never saw such a thing!'

'Oh yes you did, Mr Mayorman,' said Ogden. 'In the dress of sparkles and deepest red of cherries.'

With that, Ogden put on his pink feather boa and danced round the room, twisting and twirling, stopping only to take Willow's hand and spin her giggling across the hall in a blaze of rainbow colours.

A TALE DARK & GRIMM

ADAM GIDWITZ

Reader: beware!

Lurking within these covers are sorcerers with dark spells, hunters with deadly aim and a baker with an oven big enough to cook children in. But if you dare, pick up this book and find out the true story of Hansel and Gretel – the story behind (and beyond) the breadcrumbs, the edible house and the outwitted witch. Come on in. It may be frightening, it's certainly bloody, and it's definitely not for the faint of heart, but unlike those other fairy tales you know, this one is true.

'Gidwitz balances the grisly violence of the original Grimms' fairy tales with a wonderful sense of humour and narrative voice. Check it out!'
Rick Riordan

'*A Tale Dark & Grimm* holds up to multiple readings, like the classic I think it will turn out to be.'
New York Times

9781783440870   £6.99

The Dragonsitter

Josh Lacey
Illustrated by Garry Parsons

'Dear Uncle Morton, you'd better get on a plane right now and come back here. Your dragon has eaten Jemima. Emily loved that rabbit.'

It had sounded so easy: Eddie was going to look after Uncle Morton's unusual pet for a week while he went on holiday. But soon the fridge is empty, the curtains are blazing, and the postman is fleeing down the garden path.

'Short, sharp and funny'
Telegraph

'This witty book deserves to be read and reread'
Books for Keeps

9781849394192   £4.99